GREAT-GREAT-GREAT-GREAT GRANDMA'S RADISH AND OTHER STORIES

WELCOME TO FAIRY TALES FROM TANG TANG

Tang Tang weaves traditional Chinese storytelling with Western fantasy elements, using vivid language to craft unique stories of wonder and magic. These beautiful, poignant fairy tales will leave an imprint on your heart with their universal themes of friendship, family, loyalty and loss.

What happens when ...

- a young boy is sent to rob a silly ghost?
- a young girl faces the Blue Hag feared by everyone in the village?
- a magical radish seed sets out to do great things?
- a primary school teacher reluctantly takes a class about fairy tales?

This book is for children and for adults who never lost their sense of wonder.

EBook ISBN: 978-1-68057-306-0
Trade Paperback ISBN: 978-1-68057-306-0
Hardcover ISBN: 978-1-68057-308-4
Casebind ISBN: 978-1-68057-309-1
WordFire Press Edition 2022
Cover design by Janet McDonald
Cover artwork images by Lü Qiumei
Library of Congress Control Number: 2022935703
Published by WordFire Press, LLC
PO Box 1840 Monument CO 80132
Kevin J. Anderson & Rebecca Moesta, Publishers

CONTENTS

HIDING IN YOUR HEART

Mu Ling was seven years old when the adults first sent him to Silly Lulu Hill to bring back treasure.

Starting at the beginning of that year, the adults taught him to say four things:

"I'm cold and shivering so hard my arms are about to fall off. May I hide in your closet?"

"I'm cold and my teeth are chattering. May I rest by your fire?"

"I'm still cold. May I sleep under your blankets tonight?"

"I'm still cold. May I hide in your heart?"

Mu Ling practiced these lines from spring to summer, from summer to autumn, from autumn to winter, until he could say them quite easily.

He was a very ordinary child in Didi Village.

Near the village was a small hill called Silly Lulu Hill.

Who were the Silly Lulus? Some silly, silly ghosts.

Just how just silly? Nobody could quite say.

But adults sometimes said, "What a Silly Lulu!" if they thought their children weren't very bright.

But no matter how silly the Lulus were, no adult dared go near their hill. Those ghosts didn't like adults at all, and people said that when Lulus saw adults they got angry and did terrible things.

Silly Lulus only liked children—any children.

A mysterious and precious treasure lay in the hearts of the Silly Lulus. According to adults, there was a crystal-bright pearl in every Silly Lulu's heart.

These pearls were quite valuable.

Winter came and Mu Ling was sent on his way to Silly Lulu Hill. The night before he left, he asked fearfully, "Do Silly Lulus eat people?"

The adults laughed. "Of course not, they only eat white radishes."

"Then why don't you go yourselves?"

"Because Silly Lulus hate all adults and like all children," they replied, as patiently as they could.

"Why would they hate adults and like children?"

The adults got impatient. "How can you have so many questions? If someone hates something, they hate it. If they like something, they like it."

The sky grew lighter, but Mu Ling still hesitated. "What if I can't bring back any treasure?"

"Oh, that won't happen. All children bring back treasure, every year."

"But what if I just can't?"

"Then it would only prove how useless you are. We would be very disappointed indeed. Maybe we would even send you far, far away."

In winter, the sun was always lazy and didn't show up for a long time. Mu Ling walked through thick fog to Silly Lulu Hill. He shivered violently. As the adults wished, he was barefoot and dressed only in a thin tunic.

Mu Ling was cold. He shivered so hard he thought his bones might break.

Mu Ling was frightened. Would he get caught? Would he be eaten?

Mu Ling was curious. What did Silly Lulu ghosts look like?

He climbed the hill, shivering with each step, and entered the Silly Lulus' village, slipping like a wintry wind through the gaps between the houses.

The village was quiet. Were the Silly Lulus still warm in their beds?

He didn't know which door to knock on. He hesitated in front of this door and that. Finally, a pair of golden door-knocker rings caught his attention and he walked toward the door as if in a trance. His hands reached out and touched one of the rings.

The knocker made a sharp *dang-dang* sound, and the door creaked open.

Was that a Silly Lulu standing in front of him?

He looked like a normal human, taller than Mu Ling's father, and was dressed in a long gray robe. The robe looked as if it was stuffed full of cotton fluff, and the whole thing bulged in a rather comical way.

Well, this wasn't scary at all!

Mu Ling loved the Silly Lulu's eyes right away. He had never seen such radiant eyes, like the neon lights of a distant city. Ever so bright, with a pleasant, gentle smile.

Oh—*Light*. In his heart Mu Ling named him.

"Poor child, dressed like this on a cold day—and barefoot! You'll freeze." Light scooped him up and wrapped him in his robe. The ghost's arms felt warm and safe, and Mu Ling wished he could be hugged all the time.

But he remembered what his father had taught him.

"I'm cold and shivering so hard my arms are about to fall off. May I hide in your closet?"

Light smiled and replied, "Of course! Why not?"

He placed Mu Ling in the closet, which was full of thick coats that wrapped snugly around Mu Ling's icy form. He stayed there for a long time.

At noon Light brought him lunch. It was a small white radish.

"What is your name?"

"Mu Ling."

"Oh. Mu Ling, it's lunch time."

After finishing his lunch, Mu Ling said, "I'm cold and my teeth are chattering. May I rest by your fire?"

"Of course! Why not?" Light stretched out one long arm, scooped Mu Ling out of the closet, and placed him by the hearth. The heat of the fire warmed Mu Ling's face.

They sat together by the fire all afternoon, eating radishes: Light ate large radishes and Mu Ling ate small ones. Light crunched them loudly and Mu Ling crunched them softly.

When it was dark, Light got sleepy. The puffy ghost floated away from the fireside and went to bed.

Mu Ling said, "I'm still cold. May I sleep under your blankets tonight?"

"Of course! Why not?" The ghost smiled, got up, carried him to the bed, and tucked him under a mound of warm blankets. They slept soundly, Light drooling all over his pillow and Mu Ling following his example.

After breakfast, Mu Ling repeated the fourth saying

he had learned. "I'm still cold. May I hide in your heart?"

Light hesitated briefly, narrowed his eyes, and said, "Of course. Why not?" He hugged Mu Ling against his chest near his heart.

"Say 'Dimma Mira go into the heart,' and you'll be inside. Say 'Dimma Mira go out again' and you'll come back out," he said gently.

"Dimma Mira go into the heart," Mu Ling whispered. He knew this spell already. All at once he was cocooned in warmth and softness—he was in Light's heart. And there was a bright crystal pearl as large as an egg. He took it in both hands and said, "Dimma Mira go home."

He was home, holding a sparkling crystal pearl as large as an egg with both hands.

His parents were delighted. "This is huge," they said. "We never found pearls this large when we were kids. Well done, Mu Ling!"

Mu Ling had been feeling gloomy, but when he heard their praise, he felt proud.

Then his parents took the crystal pearl, left home in a rush, and went somewhere far away.

That winter, Mu Ling stayed at home all by himself. He was cold, so very cold.

When it was almost spring, his parents came home with a large chest of money.

Every child in Didi Village went searching for treasure at Silly Lulu Hill from the time when they were seven to the time they were eleven.

Soon winter was back, and eight-year-old Mu Ling's parents once again sent him to fetch treasure from the heart of a Silly Lulu.

As soon as Mu Ling set foot upon the hill, he ran into Light.

What could he do? Mu Ling panicked and was about to run when Light scooped him up and held him in his arms.

"It's so cold and you're wearing so little—barefoot too! You'll freeze." It was warm in Light's arms and Mu Ling did not want to leave.

"What's your name?" Light asked.

"Mu Ling."

"Oh. Mu Ling," he said. Light did not remember the boy who had stolen a pearl from his heart last winter.

Mu Ling breathed a sigh of relief. He couldn't help but look into Light's bright eyes and notice that they were dimmer now.

"I'm cold and shivering so hard my arms are about to fall off. May I hide in your closet?"

"Of course! Why not?"

Light placed him in the closet.

"I'm cold and my teeth are chattering. May I rest by your fire?"

"Of course! Why not?"

Light carried him to the fireside.

"I'm still cold. May I sleep under your blankets tonight?"

"Of course! Why not?"

Light tucked him under a pile of blankets.

"I'm still cold. May I hide in your heart?"

Light hesitated slightly. "That sounds familiar ... Oh, but of course! Why not?"

"Dimma Mira go into the heart." Mu Ling took the sparkling pearl from his heart and said, "Dimma Mira go home."

✳◌◌◌◌◌◌✳

During his ninth winter, then his tenth, then his eleventh, Mu Ling met Light. The adults told him never to look for the same Silly Lulu, but every time Mu Ling turned around, there was Light.

And every time, Light did not recognize him.

"What's your name?"

"Mu Ling."

"Oh. Mu Ling."

And every time Light gave him little white radishes to eat.

He wore a gray robe and the light in his eyes grew dimmer and dimmer.

The crystal pearls in his heart got smaller and smaller.

Mu Ling remembered his last trip into Light's heart.

The pearl he found was not much larger than a sesame seed. He winced as he took it, and a single tear slid down his cheek. He thought to himself how foolish the Silly Lulus were, and he wished that they weren't.

After Mu Ling turned eleven, he no longer went to Silly Lulu Hill. That was the rule in Didi Village. Of course there would be other children to go up the hill and find treasure, generation after generation.

From that year on, Mu Ling's heart got colder and colder. Sometimes he had to hold a hot water bottle against his chest to feel better.

A heart may be cold, but a boy must grow, and Mu Ling grew into a man.

He had a child of his own, and in the blink of an eye his child turned seven.

Soon Mu Ling would send him to Silly Lulu Hill to find treasure. He started teaching him how to talk to Silly Lulu ghosts as soon as the year began.

"I'm cold and shivering so hard my arms are about to fall off. May I hide in your closet?"

"I'm cold and my teeth are chattering. May I rest by your fire?"

"I'm still cold. May I sleep under your blankets tonight?"

"I'm still cold. May I hide in your heart?"

The same four lines as always. His son recited them from spring to summer, from summer to autumn, from autumn to winter, and learned them by heart.

And the spell "Dimma Mira go home," of course.

The night before he was going to send his child to Silly Lulu Hill, someone knocked on his door.

As soon as he opened the door, Mu Ling saw Light. As a child, he had been in Light's heart—how could he forget?

Suddenly, deep anxiety filled Mu Ling. Silly Lulus never came to the village—ever. How could they possibly come to a village where people lived? They hated all adults.

But on a night that would turn a man's breath into icicles, Light had come. What was he doing there?

They were almost the same height now, and the two of them stood astonished for a good while, one inside the door, the other outside.

Light wore his gray robe. His large eyes held no luster, like two deep wells long since dry, full of confusion and despair.

Mu Ling thought of the first time he had seen Light, how radiant his eyes had been! For a few seconds, Mu Ling felt as if something sharp had grazed his heart.

"You ... What are you doing here?"

Light said, "I'm shivering with cold. My arms feel like they're about to fall off. May I hide in your closet?"

He sounded like a young child, reciting almost the same words Mu Ling had used long ago. This had to be some sort of scheme, didn't it? Mu Ling hesitated slightly, then nodded. He wanted to see what Light would do.

Light got into the closet. He was too big for it, and some of the clothes came spilling out.

In a little while his voice came from the closet. "I'm still cold. May I rest by your fire?"

Mu Ling almost chuckled. "Of course! Why not?"

They sat by the fire. Mu Ling didn't have any radishes, so he offered Light a sweet potato, but Light waved it away. He wasn't shivering quite as badly as when he arrived. Tonight, he said, he had knocked on many doors at many houses, but each door creaked open —and just as quickly creaked shut. Nobody would let him in.

He said the wind outside was so wild that it froze the snot in his nose.

He said the Silly Lulus were going to move. For some reason, life on their hill was getting more and more unhappy, worse and worse each day. They would have to move someplace far, far away, across mountains and rivers and grasslands and deserts to the Gobi.

Mu Ling wondered how life in Didi Village would change once the Silly Lulus moved away.

Light said that there was something in his heart that had been there for more than a decade. He didn't know what it was or who had left it there, but he intended to return it before he moved ...

The night deepened, and Mu Ling went to bed.

"I'm still cold. Can I sleep under your covers?" Light asked.

Mu Ling burst out laughing. "Of course! Why not? Next you'll be asking me if you can hide in my heart for a while."

"Yes—how did you know? I'm still cold, may I hide in your heart?"

This was sounding more and more like a trick—the sort that children from Didi Village learned at age seven.

Can I let him into my heart? Mu Ling mused. *Of course not. But* why *not?*

"My heart is very cold, and it's not a good place to keep warm," he said.

Light smiled slightly. "Actually, I want to visit your heart and look inside. May I?"

"Can you get in?"

"Yes. I'm a ghost."

Then go ahead and look, Mu Ling thought. *There's no treasure beyond the endless cold.*

"Dimma Mira go into the heart," Light murmured, and then he was gone.

Was he really inside Mu Ling? His heart felt so

heavy. Mu Ling sat before the fire and waited for him to come out. He waited for many days. Nothing happened.

Why wouldn't Light come out? Was it possible that he had found something of value and whisked it away as Mu Ling had done when he was young?

But what was in Mu Ling's heart?

A week or so later, Mu Ling heard a whispered "Dimma Mira go out again," and Light stood before him.

His eyes shone as bright as the neon lights of a distant city.

"You stayed in my heart for so long." Mu Ling couldn't help but feel glad when he saw Light again. "What did you find inside? Your eyes are radiant."

"A glittering crystal pearl as large as an egg."

What? Mu Ling couldn't hide his surprise.

"That pearl holds all of your memories from childhood to adulthood."

Memories? Mu Ling's mouth fell open, and he looked rather silly.

"In your memories I saw myself."

Mu Ling's face burned red.

"Your name is Mu Ling.

"You have been to my house.

"You took five pearls from my heart, each one smaller than the last, right?

"I hugged you, didn't I? I fed you little radishes ..."

I kept all of this in my heart? Mu Ling thought. Of

course—he had never forgotten any of it. He hung his head.

"Every ghost's heart has a pearl, as does yours. Each pearl holds your memories of happiness and sadness, of ordinary days and extraordinary days. When you were young, you stole *my* memories—no wonder my heart always felt so empty, so ... awkward!"

Mu Ling hung his head even lower.

"I saw in your memories that in your mind you called me Light. I like that name. Thank you!"

At this word of thanks, Mu Ling raised his head slightly. "Do you hate me?"

"I hate that you stole my memories—how could I not? But now I'm happy, because I've found them. And more importantly, I know what it is inside my heart."

"What?"

"A tear."

A tear?

"And I know who left it there."

"Who?"

"You! The last time you were in my heart, you shed a tear. That is what stayed in my heart: your tear."

Tears flowed from Mu Ling's eyes.

"I decided not to give you back this tear. I love it. May I keep it?" Light blinked his bright, sparkling eyes.

"Yes." Mu Ling felt happy. "Of course—why not?"

Light left at daybreak, and the rest of the Silly Lulus started to move that very morning.

"Goodbye, Mu Ling!"

"Goodbye, Light!"

"It's possible we won't see each other again."

But ever since that cold, cold night, Mu Ling's heart felt warm.

KAKASHA THE WATER SPRITE

I

Tudou's big white kite fell onto the Blue Hag's roof. Xianer and the other kids told her just to leave it. Tudou hesitated for a while, then walked home feeling frustrated. The sun went down behind the mountain with a *bang,* and Sunny Valley sank into darkness.

Beside Sunny Valley lay a huge area of barren land, and in a corner of it stood a little mud hut. Leafy vines of star jasmine covered its walls, and dense spiderwebs covered the jasmine. This was where the Blue Hag lived.

Tudou had only seen her once or twice from a distance. According to local stories, she had arrived in

Nanxia Village about ten years earlier with a veil over her head and used all the money she had to buy this little hut. Someone had seen the wind raise her veil to reveal a dark, wrinkled chin, and a back ridge under her cloak. Since she looked old and wore a blue cloak, everyone called her the Blue Hag.

The Blue Hag never went out of doors, and smoke never rose from her chimney. Even after ten years, no one in the village had seen her face, much less talked with her. People didn't know where she came from or what she did, and year after year she seemed more mysterious, eccentric, and frightening. Whenever a child was naughty, parents would scare them by saying, "If you don't behave, we'll leave you on the Blue Hag's doorstep and let her eat you."

Someone had once posted a note on her door.

Whoever you are, please stay away from us.

Otherwise, don't blame us for being rude.

The next morning, the villagers found two words written in green at the bottom.

All right

And so several years had passed without further incident.

Thinking about her kite, Tudou had spent the night tossing and turning. It was barely daylight when she took a bamboo pole, went to the Blue Hag's hut, and stole softly under its eaves. It was early summer, and clusters of star jasmine blossoms were beginning to open their slender white petals. The air was rich with fragrance and all was quiet.

Tudou stood on her tiptoes. She was too small to see anything but a bit of the kite's tail sticking over the edge of the roof. She fumbled around with her pole, once, twice …

The door creaked open, and the Blue Hag leaned out.

Tudou froze from her toes to her hair. "You … you don't want to catch me … I'm not at all tasty …"

"Who said anything about eating you?" said a voice from behind the veil, surprising Tudou. She hadn't expected the Blue Hag's voice to sound sweet and smooth—not at all like an old person's, but more like the sound of murmuring water.

"I … I'm not playing a trick. My kite … is … on your roof."

The Blue Hag's feet slowly descended, and Tudou almost fainted with fear. She was close to the old woman for the first time—close enough to see that her cloak had several holes in it—and noticed a pleasant fragrance coming from her. It reminded Tudou of an aquatic plant she had smelled while wading in a stream picking water plants.

The Blue Hag held out a withered hand, palm up, fingers curved.

Tudou blinked, then understood and handed her the pole. The old woman fished the kite down with a couple of quick strokes and gave the pole back to Tudou. Then she turned, walked back into the hut, and closed the door.

With the pole in one hand and her kite in the other, Tudou started for home. Halfway there she stopped, bit her lips, and headed back to the Blue Hag's hut. Her knock on the door was so timid that she could hardly hear it.

The door opened. Above the veil, Tudou saw a pair of gentle eyes.

"I ... I forgot to say thank you."

"That's all right."

She wanted to say something else, but forgot what it was, and her face flushed. Then she remembered.

"So ... you're not an evil old woman."

"I'm not evil, just ugly."

She *was* ugly, with dark wrinkles around her eyes like trampled mud.

"Why ... why do you always stay inside and not come out?"

"Because I'm ugly, and it scares people."

"But you have a good heart."

"But the heart grows inside the body, and people can't see past the outside."

"Sooner or later they'll know that you're good."

"Most of the time they don't want to know."

"Why don't they want to know?"

"Perhaps they're not interested. Perhaps they don't have time."

This confused Tudou. She felt sorry for the Blue Hag and wondered if she had been thrown out of her home because she was so ugly. *Maybe I can make her feel a bit better.* When she got home, Tudou thought, *It's not wicked to look ugly. No one should be punished for it.*

<h1 style="text-align:center">II</h1>

Tudou knocked on the Blue Hag's door for the second time.

"It's you? Aren't you afraid of me?" The veiled Blue Hag peeked out from behind her half-open door, her gentle eyes overflowing with surprise that she couldn't hide.

"Not afraid."

"Everyone is afraid of me—why aren't you?"

Tudou wanted to say, "Because you're so pitiful," but that might hurt the old woman's feelings. So she kept quiet for a long time.

The Blue Hag said, "Thank you for not being afraid. Would you like to come in?"

"Yes, I would."

The hut was empty inside, with dried water grasses

hanging from the mud walls and covering the floor. A handful of blue-green water grass sat drying on the windowsill, so fresh it still dripped with water.

"Where is your bed?"

"I sleep on the water grass."

"Doesn't it get cold in winter?"

"I have my cloak."

Not only is she ugly, Tudou mused, *she is so poor that there probably isn't anyone more pitiful in the world.* This thought left a sour smell in her nose, and she said, "Can I bring you anything from home?"

"I don't need a thing. If you—if you would come again sometime ... I would be very happy. I am lonely and haven't talked with anyone in ten years."

"I'll come."

"What is your name?"

"Tudou."

"How can I ever thank you, Tudou? You've made me so happy—but I have nothing to give you. I've heard that children like stories, so I'll tell you a story every time you come."

Of course Tudou loved stories, so they agreed to meet every day at dusk, right after school and before dinner, which was Tudou's free time. No one would ask where she was going. The Blue Hag begged her not to tell anyone, and she agreed. Tudou looked forward to spending daily quiet time with her.

The Blue Hag's stories were about water sprites, and she told a bit every day.

"Are there really water sprites in the world?" Tudou asked.

"Yes, of course." The Blue Hag sounded certain.

"I'd really love to see one."

"I'm sure you will."

The Blue Hag refused to take off her veil, though, for fear of frightening Tudou and giving her nightmares. They sat facing each other, with the wood-framed window facing the setting sun and the water grasses sunning themselves on the windowsill, filling the room with an airy fragrance, brightness, and warmth.

III

The Blue Hag's story was long, and she spoke well, but her words came slowly, and sometimes she drifted off into a reverie, as if caught up in a long-forgotten memory. Her story continued from early summer to autumn, and it went something like this:

One hundred years ago, some water sprites came onto the shore. They had to, since the lake they were living in dried up.

The lake was called *Pululu*, which was also the name of the water sprites' language. *Pululu* meant "forever." Despite its name, it dried up.

Ten water sprites lived in Lake Pululu, and nine of them went ashore. One water sprite, whose name was Gudida, stayed in the mud near the lake center, which was still wet enough for her. She stayed behind to guard the lake. As long as one water sprite stayed, the lake would one day refill with water. If all of them left, the lake would disappear forever.

Gudida meant "brave" in their language, and she really was brave. She turned herself into a pearl, lay down in a clam shell, and made the water sprite Kakasha tie a weed all around it with her last bit of magic. The spell ensured that Gudida could never come out, no matter how much pain or loneliness she felt.

The nine water sprites who went ashore were not used to walking, and their feet soon became rough and blistered. They traveled across wild fields and forests to find crowds of people. For their own safety, they mingled with people and hid among them. Unless they stayed close to people, snakes and beasts would quickly track the water sprites by the smell of their breath and viciously attack them.

Water sprites looked much the same as humans, except for an extra crooked tooth next to their canines. These looked like a deformed human tooth and did not attract any particular attention. Because they were highly intelligent, the water sprites soon learned the language of humans and how to act like them. All nine had jobs of their own: some became bus conductors, some opened coffee shops, and one even became a kindergarten teacher. They all lived quite well.

About three years after they left Lake Pululu, however, they all developed toothaches in the extra tooth by their canines, but only on nights when there was no moon. On moonless nights, an unbearable pain spread from the extra teeth to fill their entire bodies, so that the water sprites rolled about on the floor in agony until the sun rose the next morning.

The only way to stop the pain was to pull the extra teeth out. But if they did that, they would forget all about their past, about Lake Pululu and water sprites, and become normal humans. But unlike normal people, one night when they had lived as long as a normal human does, they would turn into infants again and start a new life. There was little to be lost by removing those two extra teeth.

So one by one, the water sprites who couldn't bear the toothache pulled their extra teeth and forgot their former lives. Believing that they were human beings, they lived and ate like humans, and married and had children.

Only one water sprite did not pull her extra teeth: Kakasha. Her name meant "teardrop," which was quite fitting, because she was timid and cried easily. On nights when the moon was absent, she cried so hard that her tears soaked the bed and dripped onto the floor. Even so, she would not pull out her teeth. She didn't want to forget Lake Pululu or any of her former days, and she missed Gudida. She eagerly waited for those teeth to turn blue, which would mean that Pululu was calling out to her.

But she waited for more than a hundred years, and the color of her extra teeth did not change, meaning that Lake Pululu was still dry. Her skin changed, though. It was perfect for living underwater, but she had lived out of the water for so long that her skin dried out under the sun and became uglier than pine bark, wrinkly, dark, and rough. She often frightened people badly, and eventually she had no way to work. She went to a different village, found a house, stayed inside, and only ate a bit of water grass every day ...

IV

The story of Kakasha the water sprite fascinated Tudou. She kept asking herself, *What would I have done in Kakasha's place? Would I have pulled out those extra teeth?* Ah, Kakasha was simply amazing! Tudou admired her, adored her, and felt empathy for her, even though she was just a character in a story.

The Blue Hag always wore her veil, her gentle eyes a stark contrast with the wrinkles around them, like a stunning lake set in a field of filthy black sludge. Tudou had seen her hands—as old and rough as pine bark. The first time the Blue Hag reached out to touch her cheek, Tudou instinctively pulled back. The woman's eyes darkened, and her hand fell limp. Right away, Tudou felt bad for dodging and silently vowed never to do it again, but the Blue Hag never reached out again.

"Are there really water sprites in this world?"

"Yes."

"Then why have I never seen one?"

"Because everyone lives in their own world."

"I think Kakasha is a little silly."

"Do you think so?"

"But I also think she's amazing."

That day, when Tudou finished listening and was going home for dinner, she thought of something. "What do you eat?"

The Blue Hag's room was empty and there was no sign of food anywhere, and no pots or stoves to cook with. The Blue Hag only smiled.

The next day, Tudou was kept after school for talking in class, and when she finally dashed out of school, the last few rays of sunset were fading, and the Blue Hag thought she wasn't coming. Tudou rapped smartly on the door, and it opened to reveal the Blue Hag with bulging cheeks, holding a bundle of water grasses in one hand.

"*This* is what you eat?" Tudou asked in surprise.

"Yes, it's dinner time."

"But why would you eat water plants?"

"Because I love to eat."

"Oh—I see! You're ..."

"Yes, I am Kakasha."

"The *water sprite* Kakasha?" Tudou's mouth hung open. What word could describe her mood at the moment? Delirious? Shocked? Excited? Delighted? Yes. All of those.

"What's the matter?"

"Kakasha! Kakasha!" Tudou cried.

"Yes, what's wrong?"

"I'm so glad you're Kakasha."

"You're not afraid at all?"

"I like you, Kakasha!"

Just then, they heard Tudou's mother in the distance calling her home for dinner.

"I'll come again tonight."

"There's a bright moon tonight, so I'll be picking water grasses in the stream. See you there!"

Tudou almost told her family about Kakasha during dinner, but she managed to hold back, swallowing both her food and her story.

After dinner she excused herself, saying that she was going to catch fireflies. She ran to the stream, which was lined with wild trees and reeds, and fireflies flickered in the air.

Kakasha arrived, took off her cloak and veil, and went down into the stream. Then something magical happened.

Tudou saw a stunningly beautiful woman with fair, smooth skin, a swan-like neck, soft waist and limbs, and a back as straight as a dawn redwood.

"Oh, Kakasha, you've changed."

"Because I am in water," Kakasha replied as she fished around for grass. "This is what I really look like."

"You're so beautiful, I bet you're prettier than a fairy."

Kakasha laughed. Moonlight touched her gentle eyes, turning them a liquid blue, and Tudou could see that she really did have an extra tooth next to her canines.

She suddenly had an idea. "Kakasha, you could live in this stream."

"A stream is much too small for a lake sprite."

"There are many other lakes in this world other than Pululu."

But Kakasha said that all lakes had water sprites living in them already, and any new water sprite who wanted to live in their lake would have to obey their orders. She couldn't bear that.

She also said that she came here to pick water grass whenever there was a moonlit night, and that reeds made the best hiding place.

"Keep it secret that I am a water sprite. People don't like us to live so close to them."

"But you are a good water sprite."

But Tudou was still a child, and when Xianer one day said that the Blue Hag must be the ugliest person in the world, she couldn't keep quiet anymore. "You don't know how beautiful she is."

"Beautiful?"

"Of course. Her name is Kakasha, not Blue Hag."

"Kakasha?"

"Kakasha is a very nice water sprite."

"What—a water sprite?"

"Yes, a brave and kind water sprite. I've been listening to her stories all summer."

Xianer said, "You love making up stories. I don't believe you."

V

It rained for half a month.

There was no moonlight on rainy nights.

Without the moon, Kakasha got toothaches. Night after night was like living in hell. She begged Tudou to buy pain medicine for her, because without a job she had no money, and she had used the last of her savings to buy the hut she lived in.

Tudou bought some pain medicine and slipped out in the rain at night to be by her side. The medicine didn't work. She had to watch Kakasha writhe and moan on her bed of dried water grass, her body curled into a shaking ball.

"Have your extra teeth pulled out tomorrow."

"No."

"It would be so much better for you if you did. You wouldn't be ugly or lonely or in such pain. And you wouldn't die."

"No."

"Didn't all the others pull out their teeth?"

"I won't." Kakasha was in such pain that she couldn't speak for long. She lay panting on the dried water plants by day. Tudou helped her by collecting fresh water grass, washing it, and bringing it back.

"Thank you, Tudou."

She asked Kakasha to have at least *one* aching tooth removed.

"No. It may only be a tooth, but it's not *just* a tooth. I can't let myself forget Lake Pululu."

"You've waited a hundred years and there's still no water."

"I'll wait."

"For how long?"

"As long as needed."

Tudou couldn't imagine it—one hundred years, two hundred ... to be ugly and in pain and poor and lonely!

"Before Gudida turned into a pearl and sealed herself in a shell, she grabbed my hand and said, 'Kakasha, Lake Pululu will be full again one day and you must come home, or I'll never get out.' I promised her I would ... If I pulled out my teeth I would forget her, Tudou ... How could I not do as I promised? And you don't know how beautiful Lake Pululu was—how could I ever forget it? Not to mention, other than Gudida in the mud, I'm the only water sprite Lake Pululu has left."

"But you'll be rolling around in pain again when night comes."

"Night passes eventually. I feel fine right now."

Tudou glanced at the gloomy sky outside and gave a heavy sigh. She would not try to persuade Kakasha again.

VI

The sky cleared. Kakasha was temporarily free from her agony and continued to tell Tudou stories about Lake Pululu and the water sprites.

One evening a few days later, while one of them spoke and the other listened, they completely lost track of time.

The sun went down early, the sky's brilliant colors fading to darkness. A red-tinged crescent moon rose. They were startled by a sudden knock at the door.

Who was it? Nobody but Tudou ever knocked on that door. She opened it to see her mother and father and Xianer standing there with frightened faces. Her mother had cooked dinner and waited for Tudou to come home and eat. After waiting and waiting, she got worried. She searched for her all over the village, until she came to Xianer's house. Xianer remembered that Tudou had mentioned the Blue Hag, so the three of them had come here.

Mother pulled Tudou into her arms. Her trembling and the terror on her face frightened Tudou.

Kakasha did not show herself, and the door closed silently.

Half the village gathered in the courtyard of Tudou's home that night. It was so crowded that people could hardly find a place to stand. They all looked serious, as if something of great consequence had just happened.

They asked Tudou why she went to the Blue Hag's house, so she began to tell them about her kite landing on the roof of the hut, but the adults were too impatient to listen. In loud voices, they all tried to give their opinions at once, causing a great commotion both indoors and out.

Tudou tried to explain about Lake Pululu and the water sprites, but the more anxious she got, the more confused people were by her story.

By daybreak, the adults had arrived at their conclusion: the Blue Hag had set out to lure in a child. Therefore, the Blue Hag had to be driven away immediately.

Tudou was stunned. How had they come to that conclusion? What was the matter with them?

"Don't call her a Blue Hag! Her name is Kakasha, and she's a kind, brave water sprite ..." But the harder Tudou tried to explain, the more convinced the adults became that she was under a spell.

Surely the old woman would try to entice more and more children with her spells, the adults reasoned, and the consequences would be unthinkable. The need to get rid of the Blue Hag was already urgent.

After lunch, the autumn wind rose. Carrying hoes and sticks, men gathered on the barren ground in front of Kakasha's hut, while women and children stood on tiptoe behind them, craning their necks. Slender fruit had replaced the jasmine blossoms, and only lush, leafy vines covered the lonely mud hut.

The men pounded the ground with their hoes and sticks, making a dull *thud.*

"Come out, come out, come out, come out!"

Although her mother held her shoulder in a firm grip, Tudou shouted, "Don't come out, Kakasha, they'll beat you!"

Someone picked up a rock and threw it at the hut. More people picked up stones, and smashed them against the door, windows, walls, and roof.

"Don't throw rocks, she's a good person. She's good!"

No one paid any attention. They were too busy shouting, "Come out! Come out! Come out! Come out!"

"If you don't come out, we will burn the house down!"

The door opened slowly, just a crack, and the men in front quickly retreated, stepping on the toes of those behind them. Sticks fell, footsteps faltered, and people cried, "Ouch!" Sheepish and in disarray, the crowd watched as the veiled, blue-cloaked woman with a hunched back emerged from the hut.

"Kakasha! Tell everyone you're a good water sprite!" Tudou yelled from the back.

Kakasha's gentle eyes searched the crowd until she found Tudou and gave her a playful wink.

Again, the men beat the ground with their sticks and hoes, and the chief of the village called out through a megaphone, "If you don't leave Nanxia Village, don't blame us for being rude!"

"Yes. We will be rude!"

Their savage yells stung Tudou's eardrums. She looked around at their familiar faces. On most days, all these aunts and uncles were kind and interesting, and she liked them so much. Why were they being like this now? She was surprised and confused and sad all at the same time.

Kakasha's gaze was calm—not afraid, not sad, not angry.

The crowd suddenly fell silent.

Tudou anxiously shouted, "Tell them, Kakasha!"

"All right. I will leave tonight." These were the only six words Kakasha ever spoke to Nanxia Village, and her voice sounded as lovely as murmuring water.

Was it really so easy to chase her away? The people were rather dumbfounded, thinking they must have heard wrong. "You ... you aren't lying, are you?"

Tudou finally broke away from her mother and rushed up to Kakasha.

"Please don't leave, Kakasha—plead with them! They'll know you're good."

Kakasha shook her head.

"Why not?"

"Look at them. Nothing I say will help."

Tudou saw that it was true, and she felt guilty. "Kakasha, I told Xianer about you."

"It is nothing. You are still a child."

"Where can you go?"

"The world is so big, there is always a place to go."

"I don't *want* you to go, Kakasha."

"I don't want to go either. But we still have to say goodbye. I'll miss you, Tudou."

"I don't want to say goodbye, Kakasha ..."

The crowd dispersed, and Tudou was dragged back home. Her parents watched her all night long, and although she cried, she could not sneak out.

Early the next morning, the villagers flocked to the mud hut. The door was open, and there was no Blue Hag inside.

"She really left."

"She kept her word."

There were three words on the wooden door—

Thank you Tudou

—written in water grass juice.

Why did she thank me? Tudou wondered. *I was the one who brought all this trouble on her.*

A group of adults stood jabbering nearby. Tudou couldn't tell what they were saying, but she knew that they were beyond reason.

Can Kakasha wait until Lake Pululu calls her? Tudou looked at the wooden door and thought. *Yes, definitely. And I hope that day comes soon.*

Her eyes filled with tears, and through the blur she saw an expanse of bright blue. Was it Lake Pululu? And the two beautiful figures skipping over the ripples of water ... weren't they Kakasha and Gudida?

GREAT-GREAT-GREAT-GREAT GRANDMA'S RADISH

I. Bang-Bang-Bang-Bang

Bang-bang-bang-bang. Bang-bang-bang-bang. The strange noise, which was still going on the fifth day, was driving our family crazy.

It never halted, never changed its rhythm, like a young monk tapping his rattle, banging away from dawn to dusk and dusk to dawn.

It came from a spot beneath the glass tea table in the living room on the ground floor.

Yes, right there!

It began suddenly in the middle of the night and woke up our family. Papa and Mama dragged aside the table, and Grandpa and I pressed our ears to the floor with our backsides sticking up in the air.

Bang-bang-bang went something under the ground.

What was it?

My eyes lit up with excitement. "There must be tiny people under the floor!"

Papa also pressed his ear to the ground. "What tiny people? You think it's a fairy-tale world?"

"I'm guessing it's just a small beast down there making holes in the ground," said Grandpa sagely after holding his breath and listening for some time.

Papa and Mama nodded their agreement.

Oh? A small beast in a hole, was it? Mouse, mole, fox, rabbit? If so, what a peculiar beast it must be! Didn't it ever need to sleep or eat?

It didn't sleep, but *we* needed to.

Bang-bang-bang-bang.

We didn't sleep for four nights. Mama's eyes were puffy, with dark rings around them that no amount of eye cream could help. Papa walked about yawning endlessly, and Grandpa gave up lying in bed altogether. He simply moved a wicker chair and lay in the living room waiting.

On the sixth morning Grandpa announced his new opinion. "Maybe it's not a small beast after all."

Again, Papa and Mama nodded their agreement.

Not a small beast?

"So it *is* a tiny person under the floor!" I cried, my eyes burning with excitement.

"Could it be something terrible?" Mama asked nervously.

I saw Papa and Grandpa's thick eyebrows twitch at the same time, and for no apparent reason, a sense of foreboding flashed across my mind. I grabbed Grandpa's arm and looked into his eyes.

Slowly and calmly he said, "We are a good family. Heaven doesn't want us to be afraid! Stop thinking nonsense. If the sky falls, my old bones will be here to hold you up."

Grandpa was dressed in his usual blue shirt. His face, arms, and body were thin, and his beard and eyebrows were sparse.

If the sky comes crashing down, how can he possibly hold us up? I wondered.

He got down on the floor again with his backside in the air and pressed half of his face to the floor.

"It sounds far away, yet very close," he said after a while. "If it's not a small beast, what could it be?"

He curled his fingers and rapped on the floor three times with his knuckles. The light green floor was freshly tiled.

The *bang-bang-bang-bang* stopped unexpectedly.

"There we go." Grandpa knocked on the floor again. *Tap-tap-tap.*

The usual *bang-bang-bang* came from below.

Tap-tap-tap-tap. Grandpa knocked four times.

From under the floor came *bang-bang-bang-bang.*

Tap—tap-tap—tap-tap-tap.

Bang—bang-bang—bang-bang-bang.

Melody and harmony, suggestion and agreement.

Strangely, Papa and Mama's mouths fell open in the same "O" of astonishment. It was so rare to see them looking silly, that I couldn't help but stare.

"Wow, it *must* be a tiny person!" I was so convinced that I yelled louder than ever before.

Grandpa got up and clapped his hands together. "Let's pry up the floor tiles and dig a hole to see what's going on."

This time, Papa did not automatically nod in agreement. He said, "Dad, are you confused? We just finished fixing up the house last month. It looked awful when the floor was broken and dug up."

"Yes, simply awful," Mama agreed.

Grandpa glanced at them, and said blandly, "Well, we'll just have to put up with the banging then."

"Oh ... right. Then dig it up," Papa said despairingly.

"We'll dig it up," Mama said. After a pause, she suddenly looked nervous and tugged at Grandpa's arm. "Will ... will we dig up something dreadful? A dark cloud, or a monster, or ..."

"We are a good family, and heaven wouldn't want to frighten us." Grandpa's voice was soft and slow, and it set the other three hearts at ease.

Then it was time to get the shovel, hammer, and pickaxe.

We panted and huffed and puffed as we pried up the tiles.

We panted and huffed and puffed as we broke up the concrete.

We panted and huffed and puffed as we shoveled aside the gravel.

Strangely, the banging sound had stopped. Was it afraid? Had it run away?

We dug, dug, dug, dug to reveal the black soil.

At first, we saw nothing but a circle of dark earth.

Then, with a sound of *ch-ch-ch-ch*, a broad green leaf emerged from the soil, and came up out of the hole in the reinforced concrete. Then the second leaf, the third, the fourth.

They were bright green and shiny and full of energy, rushing up from the ground like a fountain.

What was it?

"Radish leaves," Grandpa said calmly.

"Radish leaves—" Papa's voice changed with amazement.

"Radish—leaves!" Mama screamed out loud.

"Why radish leaves?" I spoke in the same amazingly calm tone Grandpa had used. *Why couldn't it have been tiny people? How disappointing!*

But how could radish leaves grow under all this steel and concrete? It was incredible.

Even Grandpa, who had seen a lot of the world and weathered many storms, had surprise and confusion written across his thinning brows and wrinkled forehead. "This is inconsistent with the established growth patterns of radishes. So uncharacteristic of radishes," he babbled, keeping his mouth slightly open.

"This is what made all that banging?" Facing the huge bush of radish leaves, the color of Mama's fair face seemed a bit off.

Before Papa had a chance to answer, another voice spoke.

"Of course it was me! You piled a hard and heavy load on me. I knocked and knocked politely for so long before you reacted, I nearly lost my temper," the radish said in a grouchy voice, and the shiny green leaves shook their heads.

As soon as he finished speaking, two of his leaves stretched upward, straightened and—*ch-ch*—patted together twice. Several others twisted five times—*crunch* —to the left, then five times—*squeak*—to the right, and *whoosh*, released a long breath of air like a sigh.

"I'm sore and numb and numb and sore all over! Ah, I feel much better after a good stretch."

"You—what are you using to talk?" I asked in surprise.

"My radish sprouts, of course," it said smugly.

Dumbfounded, Grandpa and Papa and Mama didn't move, didn't speak a word, their mouths wide open.

The radish leaves rustled with laughter. "You look very stupid."

Grandpa quickly shut his mouth and patted his son

on the shoulder. "It's only a few radish leaves—nothing we haven't seen before. What's all the fuss?"

Papa and Mama stuck out their tongues, then shut their mouths too.

II. Great-Great-Great-Great Grandma

"I am your great-great-great-great—I have no idea how many greats—but anyway, ever so many great-great … grandma's white radish."

Great-great … grandma's radish?

"This was a vegetable garden." The radish's grouchy voice was full of disdain. "How did it become a dilapidated house?"

"Our house isn't dilapidated at all," I muttered. "We renovated just last month. Besides, this was never a vegetable garden."

But Grandpa spoke up. "Yes, it was a vegetable garden, left by our ancestors, generation after generation. Your father built a house here more than ten years ago, before you were born."

I heard the radish chuckle and my face felt hot. Its leaves had grown taller while we were talking, revealing the topmost section of its root, all white and plump.

"Please empty out your ears first," it told us solemnly.

"What?"

"I'm going to tell a story from a long, long time ago."

Upon hearing that *a radish* was going to tell a story, we quickly cleaned out our ears so as not to miss a word.

"The story took place in this former vegetable garden. What a marvelous vegetable garden it was, three hundred years ago," the radish said, sounding a bit sad.

The radish cleared its throat—*ahem-hem*—and the story began.

The heart of the story is your great-great ... grandma. I can't calculate how many—it should be several greats, maybe it's five or six, or maybe seven or eight. Anyway, your grandma from three hundred years ago. Without her, none of you would exist.

"But that's not true for me," Mama objected, and Papa glared at her.

I found her interruption a bit irritating, as well.

Your great-great ... great-grandma had a lovely name: Little Window, the clear part of the window, as in windowpane, the essence of a window. When she married into your Tang family, she was sixteen, very lively and innocent, with fine eyebrows and eyes. At the time, your great-great ... great-grandpa was twenty, and everybody called him Datang, which means Big Soup. He wasn't very good-looking, but he had a pleasant temper. He always smiled his simple, silly smile. He was obedient to Little Window—almost painfully so—and he loved her very much.

Little Window had no interest in women's work. She couldn't even make a proper shoe sole, much less weave or embroider anything. Instead, her passion was growing vegetables. She was always in her garden, either wearing a straw hat or a cloak, her little face burned dark red by the sun. I tell you, her vegetables were so fresh and tender and supple that everyone in the family loved to eat them.

As for me, I'm a radish seed she collected in her first year. I stayed in a cloth bag with a bunch of other radish seeds.

That year after the Dragon Boat Festival, Little Window sprinkled radish seeds in her garden by the handful. When the sack was empty, she breathed a long, happy sigh. Then she saw that a single black seed was stuck between her ring finger and middle finger.

That was me.

"Aha, there's one more." She shook her hand, but I refused to be dislodged. I was lying flat on my back and shamelessly clung to her with all my strength.

Little Window picked me up with two fingers, looked me over carefully, and said, "What a strange radish seed."

It's true, I was rounder and darker than the other radish seeds, and definitely more handsome. I looked at Little Window's fine, gentle eyes, and took a chance.

"Little Window."

Her eyes brightened. "Is that you, radish seed?"

"Yes! Please don't toss me aside or simply bury me in the dirt, Little Window. I am a radish seed destined to do Great Things. Don't treat me like an ordinary seed," I earnestly begged.

"Oh? Can a radish seed do Great Things?" Little Window was surprised, her eyes glimmering like stars.

"You don't believe me?" I asked anxiously.

"Well, it's a bit unbelievable unless you can tell me what you're going to do." She placed me on her warm palm.

"Of course I can't tell you—I have to keep it secret until I've done it," I said firmly.

"In that case, I'll ignore you." Little Window raised her chin and hid her face.

I grew frantic, and so did my words. "Window, oh, Window! No one else in the world can help me. If you don't believe me, no one will believe me!"

She still didn't look at me, but she pursed her lips and giggled hard.

I continued. "Please, you must believe that I am an extraordinary radish seed. I'm going to do big, big things —things no other radish in the world could accomplish, from thousands of years in the past to thousands of years in the future."

"Is it really *that* big a deal?" Little Window's eyes widened as she stared at me once more.

"Really. I'm not lying to you."

"All right then—how can I help you?" she asked, tilting her head.

I asked her to dig me a hole thirty feet deep.

"That deep? That will be a very difficult thing." She furrowed her delicate brow. "And when I'm done?"

"Put me in and I'll sleep soundly for three hundred years."

"Three hundred years?" she exclaimed.

"Yes. After sleeping for three hundred years I'll have enough power to do incredible things."

"But my eyes will be long closed by then. How will I know if you told the truth?" Little Window exclaimed.

"Because," I shouted excitedly, "I'm not just a radish that can do Great Things, I'm also a radish that matters."

"But I can't seem to get interested in things I'll never see," she said softly.

At her words my vision went dark. Why must it be so difficult for a radish to do Great Things? I couldn't help crying. *Wah-wah-wah!*

"What's wrong, radish seed?"

"I'm crying."

"Don't cry, okay?"

"I don't know what else to do."

"But when you cry my heart gets—*squeak*—soft and —*squeak*—sad. It's so uncomfortable."

I was making her heart all soft and sad? I began to cry even harder, and I sang, "Oh, I am a sad radish seed, oh, I'll always be a sad radish seed. *Wah-wah-wah!*"

"Okay, okay! I'll help you."

My crying abruptly stopped.

Your great-great ... grandmother was a woman with a soft heart, as soft as marshmallows.

Little Window went to get your great-great ... grandpa Datang.

"What is it, Little Window?" he asked, smiling.

She held out the palm of her hand. "See this radish seed?"

"Oh, a radish seed," Datang said. "It's very dark and round—why don't you plant it?"

"He's not just any radish seed. He's going to grow into a radish that will do Great Things," she said.

Datang burst out laughing, showing his big white teeth. "You're so cute, Little Window!"

"You must help me dig a hole thirty feet deep."

"To do what?"

"Plant a radish."

"No need. Radish seeds will rot if they are buried too deep."

"Didn't I just tell you that he's not an ordinary radish seed? He is meant to do Great Things!" Little Window's face always flushed a bit when she got upset.

Datang laughed so hard he couldn't close his mouth. "Little Window, oh, Little Window, you are adorable! You're always so imaginative!"

"I'm not imagining anything. The radish seed told me personally."

"*Ha-ha-ha-ha-ha!*" Datang squatted down, still chuckling.

"Oh, stop laughing! Will you help me or not?" Little Window's face turned very red, and she huffed with anger.

"Do you really want to dig a thirty-foot hole for a radish seed? It sounds ridiculous. We'll be laughed at." Datang finally managed to rein in his laughter. He'd give himself a stomachache if he laughed any harder. "When will this radish seed do something great?"

"In three hundred years."

"What? *Ha-ha-ha!*" Datang finally sat on the ground as he laughed.

"I gave the radish seed my word," Little Window said, stamping her foot. "Anyway, if you don't help me dig, I'll be angry with you, I'll stop talking to you every day, and I won't eat or drink."

And then ...

Your great-great ... great-grandpa and your great-great ... great-grandma got up early every morning and dug in the garden, digging for a whole month until they had a hole thirty feet deep.

Little Window's hands were covered with calluses.

On their last day of digging, a jade bracelet on Little Window's wrist accidentally hit the handle of a hoe, cracked into several pieces, and fell into the hole with a clatter.

Datang had brought that bracelet home for Little Window from a village far, far away. It was precious, and it was Little Window's favorite piece of jewelry.

Datang was upset and gently scolded her for her clumsiness.

Little Window, who was already sad, burst out crying when he blamed her.

Seeing his wife cry, Datang immediately panicked and tried to comfort her. "What is so important about one jade bracelet? I'll buy you ten or twenty if you like."

Little Window shook and sobbed and finally cried herself out. When she stopped, she wiped her eyes and gently threw me into the hole.

"Goodbye, radish seed that will do Great Things."

So I slept happily in the dark world, slept and slept to this day.

"Without your great-great ... grandma, where would I be today?" the radish said gratefully.

The story ended there, and our family was deeply immersed in the story of our great-great-great-great-grandma.

Ah, what a lovely grandmother we had! A grandma willing to dig a thirty-foot hole for a radish seed was indeed marvelous. Strangely, I thought of her as about my age, even though she had so many "greats" in front of her. She seemed to be very close to me—not three hundred years away.

III. The Radish That Does Great Things

"So what is the Great Thing that you will do?" I asked eagerly.

"I have to keep it secret until I finish it," Radish replied, just as it had to my great-great ... great-grandma three hundred years ago.

I stuck out my tongue in frustration, and I could see that my parents were quite upset too.

Grandpa laughed. "Don't try to force it. When someone doesn't want to talk there's always a reason."

The radish poked out two of its leaves and shook Grandpa's hand. I quickly reached out my own hand, and he shook it as well. His leaves felt cool and prickly and itchy all at once.

"All right, then—I'm going to start doing Great Things, start achieving the great ideals of a radish. You will help me, won't you?" the radish asked in a trembling voice.

I was the first to cry out, "Of course!"

Grandpa nodded and assured the radish, "We will."

Papa and Mama looked at each other and said, "We will."

The radish's voice grew shakier with excitement, which is always expected before doing Great Things. He said, "You are all as kind and lovely as your great-great... great-grandmother."

We were giddy with happiness at this heartfelt compliment from a radish. It was an amazing feeling.

"Now please break up this hard and heavy floor and move all your things out of the house as soon as possible."

"Why?"

"Because I am going to grow big—big enough to knock down these walls and break through the roof."

Taken aback, Mama screamed, "That won't work!"

"Well, no," Papa said, shaking his head.

Grandpa sighed. "Let us think it over."

I shook my head like a rattle. "No, no, no."

"Didn't you all just agree to help me?" The radish sounded hurt.

"How could we know that you'd make such an outrageous request?" Mama sounded quite angry. She and her father had built this house brick by brick, and it held more than a dozen years of her memories, both sweet and sour. No wonder she was upset.

"We cannot help you with this favor. I am sorry," Papa said as calmly as he could.

I looked at Grandpa, who frowned but didn't speak.

"But you promised," the radish muttered. "I'll wither and die soon if you don't help me. I've waited for three hundred years, gathering strength, building up the passion in my heart. I cannot accept this. Why is it so difficult for a radish to do Great Things?"

The radish began to wail—*wah!*—like wind through a barren forest on a wintry night.

My heart grew—*squeak*—soft and—*squeak*—sad.

Grandpa took us outside and held a family meeting. The subject was, "Faced with a radish about to do Great Things, should we help or not?"

"Not." Mama was adamant.

"Don't rush to answer," Grandpa said. "Think it through. What is the result of helping? What is the result of not helping?

"If we help, we will lose our house but fulfill the dream of a radish. Ask yourself how many people in the world are lucky enough to meet a radish who does big things? It is something no one has done before, and no one will do again.

"If we don't help him, we will still own a house, but we'll let a magical radish die with his dreams unfulfilled. We will miss a once-in-a-lifetime experience. Wouldn't that be a pity?

"What Great Thing is this weird radish supposed to accomplish?" Papa muttered to himself.

"I really want to know," I blurted.

He looked at me. "Wouldn't it be foolish?"

Everyone hesitated.

Grandpa suddenly said in a loud voice, "On the other hand, what if we do one foolish thing today? If it is foolish at all."

We all knew what he meant, and Mama said, "But where will we live if we don't have a house?"

"I'll think of something," Grandpa said, stroking his sparse beard.

My mind was full of this magical radish, and my heart was bursting with curiosity. I said, "Grandpa, do you think our great-great ... great-grandma would want us to help?"

"Think about it," he said. "Back in the day, she dug a hole thirty feet deep just because a radish seed spoke to her. You tell me—would she want us to help?"

"Of course she would," I answered simply.

Grandpa clapped his hands together. "Then let's help this radish today."

Papa did not speak at first. His expression made it clear that he was struggling with a difficult choice. He always listened to his father, however, and since Grandpa had made up his mind, Papa raised no more objections.

Mama kept silent. She always listened to Papa.

Before going back in the house, Papa said, "To tell the truth, I really want to see what Great Things a radish can do."

Mama said, "Me too."

So our entire family walked to the radish.

Grandpa said, very earnestly, "We will help you."

The radish laughed—*rustle-rustle-rustle*—and when he finished he said with great emotion, "Your hearts are as soft as your great-great ... great-grandmother's, as soft as marshmallows."

The television, fridge, washing machine, sofa, bed, and table ... all were moved outdoors. The potted plants from the balcony, the wedding photo on the wall, the patterned calico curtains—Mama forgot nothing. The two-story house was completely empty.

Mama's tears came all of a sudden, bringing dismay to Papa's face.

Grandpa and I closed our lips tightly and moved everything a good thirty feet away from the house, as Mr. Radish had requested.

Then, Grandpa and Papa swung their sledgehammers and smashed the living-room floor.

They were halfway finished when the radish said, "Okay, I am ready. I have enough strength. Go ahead and run."

Papa and Grandpa ran out with sweaty faces and stood near the furniture and appliances, watching our house from a distance. After a huge *crunch-crack-rattle* sound, the house began to shake and cracks climbed the walls, twisting like snakes. With a *bang-bang-boom*, the roof broke, tiles falling everywhere. Then the entire house twisted and collapsed at the base of an enormous radish.

Yes, an enormous radish. It was carrot-shaped, with emerald green leaves and a fat white body, wider and taller than our house had been!

Mama was about to cry again when she saw the radish, and stood stupefied, her tears and sorrow all but forgotten.

My admiration for the radish was so great that I ran up to him and opened my arms for a hug. The surface was cool and hard and when I tapped it with my fingertips it felt as if it was carved out of Chinese white jade. No wonder it had broken through the roof so easily. This was extraordinary.

"Big radish, are you going to start doing Great Things?" I shouted up to him.

"Shh. Don't talk," Mr. Radish said.

Then he stood alone and ignored us.

Our eyes were reluctant to look away and we gazed at him until our necks were sore. Darkness came down like the lid of a large pot.

The evening wind blew and the radish leaves, which were spread out like a giant umbrella, remained motionless. Above him, groups of stars came out to stroll.

"The weather is good," Grandpa said. "There are stars, there's a cool breeze, and it's quite comfortable. Let's just lie in the open air tonight."

So we lay down on our beds beneath the sky, and I faced the stars for a while. A delicate luster emanated from the green radish leaves, as if they were carved from jade.

Mama said it was wonderful to sleep under the stars. After a short while, the worry on her face quietly receded, and when she smiled, the light of the stars fell into her eyes.

We all fell asleep and were awakened halfway through the night by the sudden splattering of rain.

We were fumbling around looking for umbrellas when the radish said in a trembling voice, "Hey, the Great Thing I needed to do is done."

His words immediately made us forget our irritation and we pricked up our ears to listen.

"What is your 'Great Thing'?" Grandpa and I asked eagerly.

The radish trembled more and more, and I could understand his joy and excitement.

"Oh, my heart is about to leap out! I can't believe that I so quickly did something that I have been waiting to do for more than three hundred years."

"Well, what is it?" Our family, under umbrellas now, craned our necks and shouted to him, while raindrops pelted our eyes. They fell thicker and faster, drenching everything. Papa and Mama brought an umbrella forward, so raindrops fell on half of his plump body.

"A big white bird just perched on my shoulder and rested for a while," he said happily.

"But what was the Great Thing you just did?" Grandpa pressed.

"That was it—letting a big white bird rest on my shoulder for a while," the radish repeated happily.

"What?" The four of us stood open-mouthed and wooden in the rain.

"How is *that* a Great Thing?" I demanded after returning to my senses.

Papa and Mama hung their heads and let their umbrellas tilt to one side. The rain soaked them.

Still delighted, the radish said, "For a radish, of course, this is a Great Thing. It is the Great Thing I set out to do! How many other radishes in the world have had a big white bird stop and rest on their shoulders? Absolutely none."

"We did a really Foolish Thing," Papa said dejectedly.

Grandpa, who was still craning his neck, mumbled, "This is indeed a Great Thing—*for a radish*, alas."

Mama turned her head and gave him a reproachful look.

All my admiration for the radish vanished without a trace.

In the morning, the rain stopped and the red sun shone tenderly on our embarrassed family. At the foot of the huge radish stood our ruined house.

Grandpa led us in cleaning up our things. "The matter is over now. What's the use in being sad?" he asked. "There will be a way. Anyway, it is a privilege to be able to see so large a radish."

He had hardly mentioned the radish when the radish gave a long sigh, like a brisk wind blowing down a long alleyway. He said, "Suddenly I have no dream, and I feel very empty. My body is empty. Forget it. I'll be your house. Hurry up and make a door in me first."

Could a radish become a house?

Unconvinced, Mama ran over and pounded vigorously on the wall. "It's white jade!" she exclaimed in delight.

Inside, the radish was indeed huge and empty. We laughed and danced inside his belly.

"Satisfied?" the radish asked.

"More than satisfied!" we said in unison.

We moved one thing after another into the enormous radish: the wedding photos of Mama and Papa, the curtains—Mama forgot nothing.

"You see how it is?" Grandpa said. "We are a good family, and heaven didn't want us to suffer."

Papa and Mama called in craftsmen, and in a few days we were living in a beautiful radish villa, the only one in all the world.

I'll tell you a secret. For a long time after this, people came to our door, hoping to buy this wondrous mansion. The prices they offered went from one or two million up to ten million. But of course no amount of money could interest us. It was such a beautiful villa.

When it was late at night and quiet all around, the radish would tell affectionate stories of our great-great ... great-grandma. Sometimes he sighed sweetly like the wind, "*Whoooo*—who would have thought I would become a house? This is truly a Great Thing."

One day, in the most deserted corner of the radish villa, I happened upon a jade bracelet cracked into several pieces, a curve of pale green like a warm smile. I knew it must have belonged to our great-great ... great-grandma Little Window.

She seemed to be so very close, pursing her lips and watching us with a secret smile.

CREATIVE TALK: CHASING THE ROAD TO FAIRY TALES

Looking back on it, my journey as a writer began seventeen years ago.

Because I had written several short essays as dry as tofu skins, Mr. Xu Zhiyang, a children's literature enthusiast from my hometown, suggested, "You might as well write children's literature."

"But I'm not interested," I answered him frankly.

In August 2003, Professor Jiang Feng held a children's literature workshop in our small Wuyi county.

Because of the high heat and summer vacation, I was more than ready to play hooky. However, our principal announced that every Chinese teacher was required to be present, and attendance would be taken. So I bit the bullet and reluctantly went to class.

Life is filled with chance, and various possibilities

are always brewing. I developed a lasting interest in children's literature simply because of those lessons, and it was as if a window had opened before me. It turned out that children's literature was not the childish, naïve, cajoling stories I had always imagined it to be. In classic children's literature the warmth of prose, deep thinking, penetrating emotion, and story tension can reach right into the soul.

On the day the class ended, I could hardly rein in my impulse. I recorded my thoughts in a piece called "Perhaps a New Beginning." I planned to start writing fairy tales in my spare time and read them to children.

It was such a simple, straightforward idea. That was it. I began to write children's literature. I never imagined I would turn into a fairy tale author.

As a rough cut, my development as a creator of fairy tales can be divided into several sections.

2003–2006: The Budding Stage
of Fairy Tale Creation

I rarely mention any works from this time period—I don't even like people to see them. They are something of an embarrassment. Actually though, each one was a sincere step on my road of learning to write fairy tales. Every footstep was necessary, and every terrible work was necessary and valuable to me.

2007: Getting the Feel of Fairy Tale Writing with "Waiting for You with Eighteen Eggs"

While listening to a class at school one day, my mind wandered back to a little hen I raised as a child, a creature with a unique temperament. She didn't sleep in the henhouse at night but liked to sit dreaming on the windowsill. Sometimes she jumped on my shoulders or head and accidentally pooped there. We were so close that I raised her as if she were a pet, letting her stand on one shoulder as I strutted proudly around the village. I can't remember if she laid eggs anymore, but I do remember that she went missing one day, and never appeared again. It became a childhood mystery. I waited for her, and even now I find myself wondering where she went.

Inspiration struck. I wrote in the breaks between classes and grading homework. My hands danced as I wrote. When I was done, I couldn't wait to read it to the children. They listened, laughing and laughing, and then went quiet. I looked up to see some children wiping their eyes and others still crying. That was right. That was the effect I wanted to have. I ran a lap around the playground in my exhilaration. I could hardly contain my happiness, knowing I had written something wonderful, better than anything I had written before.

"Waiting for You with Eighteen Eggs" gave me a

strong sense that I had found the *feel* of writing fairy tales and might become an excellent fairy-tale author. My stories would be read by many people! I decided to use a pen name and began mulling it over. My surname is Tang, so why not Tang Tang? It sounds nice if you say it once, and even nicer if you say it ten times in a row. Children would remember it once they heard it and couldn't forget even if they wanted to. So it was a happy decision, with a thread of ambition woven into it, as well: Tang Tang—pronounced "shangshang"—can also mean a rushing river, carrying a subtle hint of my hopes and dreams.

2007–2020: The Indefinite Rise

During this time I wrote mainly stories of ghosts and gods, short and happy stories, fantasy childhood stories, and fantasy stories in which my imagination ran wild. I also wrote "Classes for Beasts" and "The Green Pearl."

I'll focus first on my ghost fairy tales, since people often joked that I achieved overnight success writing them. A journalist from *Chinese Readers' Weekly* once speculated that before Tang Tang's ghost fairy tales, it was unthinkable to make a ghost the main character in a fairy tale. But from Tang Tang's pen, ghosts became living characters, full of childlike qualities and emotion. They could be romantic, sad, or mischievous, their hearts often filled with a richer, more enduring love than the hearts of the living. People couldn't help but wonder if the author who created these poor, lovable, detestable beings hadn't grown up listening to ghost stories.

Of course not. I rarely watch horror films or listen to ghost stories. I can't endure that feeling of terror. I am a timid person.

So they ask, "Then what made you think of using ghosts as a main point of view in your fairy tales?"

Yes, why? I've asked myself why I don't use rabbits, dogs, cats, mice, badgers, or moles as main characters in fairy tales. I don't know why exactly, I just know that those words never make my heart feel anything new, but when I suddenly collide with the word "ghost," my heart stirs and comes alive, as if a story just has to come out.

Late one night, when my husband was driving and I was in the back seat, there was a moon and wind and trees on either side. The trees swayed in the wind and cast shadows in various shapes and poses on the windows. I was so sleepy and dazed that I felt as if I was in a trance and the spirits of the world were haunting me. *Spirits?* Spirits are foreign, but ghosts can be Chinese. *Ghosts?* Why shouldn't I write fairy tales about ghosts?

In my excitement I tried rather incoherently to share the idea with my husband.

He said, "Ghosts? Don't scare the children. And

why would anyone read a ghost fairy tale? Fairy tales are so beautiful—are ghosts really appropriate?"

I didn't care whether they were "appropriate" or not. I felt an urgent need to tell stories, and my heart was bursting with creative passion. I didn't care if I wrote stories and nobody wanted to read them.

So I started writing, writing all about those unique, charming, wistful, mischievous, lovely, kind ghosts, writing one after another: a ghost in a jasmine trench coat, a carved wooden bed ghost, ghosts called Evening Cry and Windfall, ghosts at Silly Lulu Hill, ghosts in Wooden Knob Cave ... I was immersed in my imagination all day long, immersed in the bliss of weaving stories. Yes, it was just about the happiest time I've had writing, a time when I wrote smoothly and heartily.

It must have been a gift from heaven that I could turn things most children feared into wonderful dreams, giving them a stunning and satisfying reading experience again and again. When I write about ghosts, I am in fact writing about human nature, about human feelings, about the world, about the loneliness and sorrow of life, about my perceptions of life and the world.

My first book ever was published in January 2010—actually two books at the same time: the long fairy tale *Jiujiu from Ghost Manor* and a collection of shorter stories, *Hiding in Your Heart*. I'll never forget the day in 2009 when an editor told me in a QQ instant message that my ghost stories would be published. The joy of that moment was so overwhelming, I didn't know what to do with it. It felt as if a string of fireworks went off inside my small heart and left my heart sore. Later I walked alone along the river for a long, long time, and laughed to myself a long, long time to release that joy. Happiness, like sorrow, can leave internal wounds if you don't let it out.

Those kind, sad, poetic, lovely, mischievous, romantic ghosts plunged my heart into the impulse and happiness of storytelling for two or three days. While writing the ghost fairy tales, I gained a certain creative perspective: I wanted my fairy tales to be unique and fascinating, to have meaning and context, to be told in words that shine with simple brilliance, to tell a story so quiet and deep or so thrilling that it would draw the reader to finish in one sitting. Afterward, the story would echo in the soul. Readers would smile or sigh, feel empowered and inspired, or leave with their hearts softer, more pure. This view of creation has not changed for me over the years, though I can't always achieve it.

One of the deepest feelings I had at the time was that the story you are about to write should appeal to *you*. For me, the stories I make up, the mood I create, the things I want to express must first fill me with passion before I can write them down. I can't force myself.

So what attracts me? I must first move myself. I must experience a constant sense of surprise and freshness in the process of conceptualizing and "brewing." Ultimately, if there is no desire to tell a story, it cannot be written by perseverance and persistence alone. Only a full-blown narrative urge gives birth to a fairy tale with its full lifeblood. Every time I finish a fairy tale, I feel emptied out. After pouring out all thoughts and emotions, there is a feeling of excitement and collapse. Writing a good fairy tale requires that you give it your all every time.

At that time, I found a pattern. Works that are strenuous and deliberate are often bad, while works that flow smoothly and easily may be masterpieces. Before I begin each work, I subconsciously hope that it will be a good story, but after too many attempts that went wrong, I eventually stopped expecting it.

I once wrote in my diary, "I think that if I keep writing this way, there will always be some good works born, even if it's only one in ten or one in a hundred." Whenever inspiration flashed—a word, an artistic concept, or a rough germ of a story appearing in my mind—I quickly grabbed them and mulled them over again and again. Some of them became complete stories, while others just faded away.

I am not a particularly talented person. I have few enough inspirations that I cherish each one and treat it kindly. I grasp them quickly, but I do not use the pen easily. I work them over and over in my mind into all sorts of possibilities, choose the most natural and sensible way of telling the story, then start slowly and write slowly.

Sometimes the inspiration for a story does not come for a long time, so I take the initiative and look for it. When I search for a story, it often looks like this: I wake up in the morning, go out walking on the road, and think about it. My eyes may not seem to look at anything, but I'm looking at everything. I may look at the sky for a while, at the ground for a while, at a stone for a while. Looking at a tree, my whole body and soul seem to be concentrated into an arrow, always ready to aim at a place where the next story lies, and like the tentacles of an octopus, I stretch out in all directions to capture inspiration. My experience is that when you concentrate on waiting and looking for inspiration, your mind becomes extremely keen. No matter what you see or hear or what flashes through your mind, you can quickly catch it and make judgments about whether it is suitable for a story.

I know that I'm lucky to have found something I love from the bottom of my heart—writing fairy tales for children. I have quietly and seriously asked myself two questions: First, do children really need fairy tales? And second, do children need to read the fairy tales *I* write?

First, there is no question that children need fairy tales. They plant truth, goodness and beauty, imagination and creativity, in the mind at a young age. They sow purity, innocence and softness, rich emotion, and curiosity about the world. Hearts nourished by good fairy tales grow up to be kinder and more powerful and have the ability to live happy lives.

But the second question—whether children need to read *my* fairy tales—has a rather keen edge. If I answer yes, I must be arrogant. If I answer no, then why do I write them? I know well enough that my works are only a drop in a vast sea of literature, comparatively weak and small. Most children in the world will never get to know the books I wrote. On the other hand, some children *will*. Isn't *that* the source of value and meaning in my writing? Let the children who meet my stories by chance not be disappointed. Let the eyes of these encounters brighten a little, let their hearts be moved, swept away, and touched for a moment, polished, warmed, and even deeply shocked. When they close my book, let them sigh happily and say, "Good, this book by Tang Tang did not waste my precious time." Yes, I dream of using all my love and wisdom to write fairy tales that leave a little warmth, brightness, and beauty behind in the hearts of children.

What story will I write next? I don't know. Even I am curious about it.

What I know is that I have an entire land of fairy tales, and I am the king of my own kingdom. I can be more capricious, bolder, let go of all rules and restraints and write in whatever way suits me best, following my storytelling impulses. I can write stories that other people can't write or can't think of, write stories in places where there seems to be no story, let my imagination open its teeth and spread its claws in places that seem exhausted, write to surprise people and make them say, "I didn't realize you could write about this, but this is how it can be done ..."

PUBLISHER'S NOTE

The original text of this work was created in Chinese. The translator, editor, and publisher have made every effort to ensure that the English-language version is as accurate as possible and in keeping with the artistic intent of the author. Because this work reflects a different culture, some of the ideas and attitudes may be unfamiliar to the English-language audience.

ABOUT THE AUTHOR

Tang Tang, one of China's most celebrated authors of children's literature, began creating fairy tales in 2003. Her works often integrate traditional Chinese storytelling with Western fantasy elements, using vivid and humorous language to craft unique stories of wonder and magic.

She is a member of the Chinese Writers Association (and one of its first "National Reading Promoters"), vice chair of the Zhejiang Writers Association, and image spokesperson for reading in Zhejiang. Tang Tang has won numerous children's literature awards in China, including the Gold Award, and the National Outstanding Children's Literature Award—China's highest award in the field—for three consecutive years.

Among her best known works are "Hiding in Your Heart," "Kakasha the Water Sprite," "A Biography of the Incisor A Shang," and "Green Pearl." Her works have been translated into English, Japanese, Russian and many other languages.

www.ingramcontent.com/pod-product-compliance
Lightning Source LLC
Chambersburg PA
CBHW061127100726

47911CB00013B/718